But there is something else extra special about Little Miss Hug's hugs.

It is her extra special arms.

They fit perfectly around whoever she is hugging.

Whether it is Mr Small after a twig fell on him and squashed his hat.

Or Mr Bump after one of his bumps.

Or even Mr Greedy when he has a tummy ache.

Little Miss Hug is always there with a perfectly fitting hug to make everything better.

Then there are times when nobody has hurt themselves.

Happy times like birthdays.

Everyone wants a birthday hug!

And times when she hugs just for the fun of it.

Even the likes of Little Miss Bossy need a hug once in a while.

So, everyone needs a hug.

Or so Little Miss Hug thought.

The other day when she was out for a walk, she heard someone hidden on the other side of a hedge.

Someone huffing and puffing and moaning and groaning.

Someone who was in a very bad temper.

Mr Grumpy!

And why was Mr Grumpy in such a bad mood?

Because the sun was out!

There really is no pleasing Mr Grumpy.

Quick as a flash, Little Miss Hug ran round the hedge, stretched out her arms and hugged Mr Grumpy.

Or at least she tried to, but something happened that had never happened to Little Miss Hug before.

Mr Grumpy pushed her away.

"Get off me!" shouted Mr Grumpy.

Little Miss Hug could not believe her ears.

She could not believe her eyes.

Nobody had ever refused one of her hugs!

"But … but, everyone likes a hug!" she cried.

She was so confused she hugged Mr Grumpy again.

"I know what you are trying to do," said Mr Grumpy. "But it won't work. I am grumpy and I like being grumpy and no amount of hugging will change that."

Little Miss Hug didn't let go.

"I said…" began Mr Grumpy, but then he stopped.

Something was happening to Mr Grumpy that had never happened to him before.

He could feel a strange, warm feeling spreading out from deep inside him.

Little Miss Hug hugged him tighter.

And then the most extraordinary thing happened.

Very slowly, Mr Grumpy smiled.

For the first time in his life, he was happy.

Little Miss Hug let go of him.

"I must say," said Little Miss Hug. "You have a lovely smile."

And can you guess what Mr Grumpy did next?

He blushed!

For the first time in his life, he blushed.

And then he hugged Little Miss Hug.

For the first time in his life he hugged someone!

Although, as you can see, it was almost a hug, not a proper Little Miss Hug hug.

What you might call…

…half a hug!

A Mr Grumpy hug.